For my father
—A.S.C.

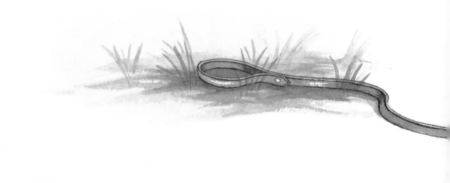

Biscuit Takes a Walk Text copyright © 2009 by Alyssa Satin Capucilli Illustrations copyright © 2009 by Pat Schories All rights
reserved. Manufactured in China. No part of this book may be used or reproduced in any manner whatsoever without written
permission except in the case of brief quotations embodied in critical articles and reviews. For information address HarperCollins
Children's Books, a division of HarperCollins Publishers, 195 Broadway, New York, NY 10007. www.icanread.com
Library of Congress Cataloging-in-Publication Data is available.
ISBN 978-0-06-117745-3 (trade bdg.) — ISBN 978-0-06-117746-0 (pbk.)

14 15 16 17 18 SCP 10 9 8 7 6 ❖ First Edition

I Can Read!

SHARED My First READING

Biscuit Takes a Walk

story by ALYSSA SATIN CAPUCILLI
pictures by PAT SCHORIES

HarperCollins*Publishers*

Time for a walk, Biscuit.

Woof, woof!

It's time for a walk
to Grandpa's house.

Let's go!

Woof, woof!

Time for a walk, Biscuit.

Woof, woof!

Biscuit wants to dig.

Time for a walk, Biscuit.

Woof, woof!

Biscuit wants to roll.

Funny puppy!
It's time for a walk
to Grandpa's house.

Let's go!

Woof, woof!

Time for a walk, Biscuit.

Woof, woof!

Biscuit wants to see

the squirrels.

Time for a walk, Biscuit.

Woof, woof!

Biscuit wants
to see the birds.

Silly puppy!
It's time for a walk
to Grandpa's house.
Woof!

Wait, Biscuit. Come back.

Grandpa's house is this way!

Woof, woof!

Oh, Biscuit!

What do you see now?

Woof, woof!

It's Grandpa!

Woof, woof!

A walk to Grandpa's house

is fun, Biscuit.

But a walk with Grandpa

is the best walk of all.

Time for a walk, Biscuit.

A walk for everyone.

Woof, woof!